THE ADVENTURES OF S
ILLUSTRATED ANI

CW01646906

BOOK 2

# The Red-Headed League

*By* Arthur Conan Doyle

*Illustrated by* Sidney Paget

*Annotated by* George Cavendish

Solis Press

## THE BOOKS IN THIS SERIES




*Photo credits*: cover and internal images




This edition is based on the complete *Adventures of Sherlock Holmes* published by Solis Press in 2014 (ISBN 978-1-910146-08-8). The individual annotated stories were first published as ebooks in 2011 by Solis Press.





ISBN: 978-1-910146-51-4

Published by Solis Press, Tunbridge Wells, Kent, England

*Web*: www.solispress.com | *Twitter*: @SolisPress

# EDITOR'S INTRODUCTION

*The Red-Headed League* is the second of Arthur Conan Doyle's 56 short stories that were published in *The Strand Magazine* between 1891 and 1892.

Conan Doyle had introduced Sherlock Holmes, the consulting detective, in his first novel, *A Study in Scarlet* published in 1887, and then again in *The Sign of Four* published in 1890. It might be fair to say that it was not until the serialization of Conan Doyle's stories in *The Strand Magazine* that the public's imagination was caught by the accounts of Sherlock Holmes's cases. Indeed, the magazine was extremely popular at the time: circulation was at around 500,000 copies a month through to the 1930s.

In *The Red-Headed League*, the second of the twelve short stories that make up *The Adventures of Sherlock Holmes*, the narrative is taken up as usual by Dr. John Watson, who was Holmes's friend and confidant. Watson acted as an unofficial biographer, and in the story we read his account of the case.

The character of Watson was introduced in the very first book as a British army doctor who had been discharged from active duty in Afghanistan after suffering a gunshot injury. Watson was searching for a place to live in London and met Sherlock Holmes who too was in need of accommodation. They decided to share the expense of lodging in 221b Baker Street. After living in Baker Street, Watson moved away when he married. In this story he is reminiscing with his old friend.

The text is close to that as first published. I have edited some of the spellings, so that they are the ones more commonly used nowadays, otherwise the text is unaltered.

As the story was written over 120 years ago, I felt that some explanation was needed to help those readers who are not familiar with some of the phrases used by the author and his characters. Some phrases are still in use in modern-day British English, but I have attempted to describe some of these to make the text clearer to English speakers from outside of the UK, or to those who do not speak English as a first language. I have also included some background information on places, names and terms used in the story.

It is not essential to consult the notes when reading this book. However, I hope that my explanations will enhance the reader's enjoyment of this story by giving them some insights that might otherwise have been missed.

*George Cavendish*

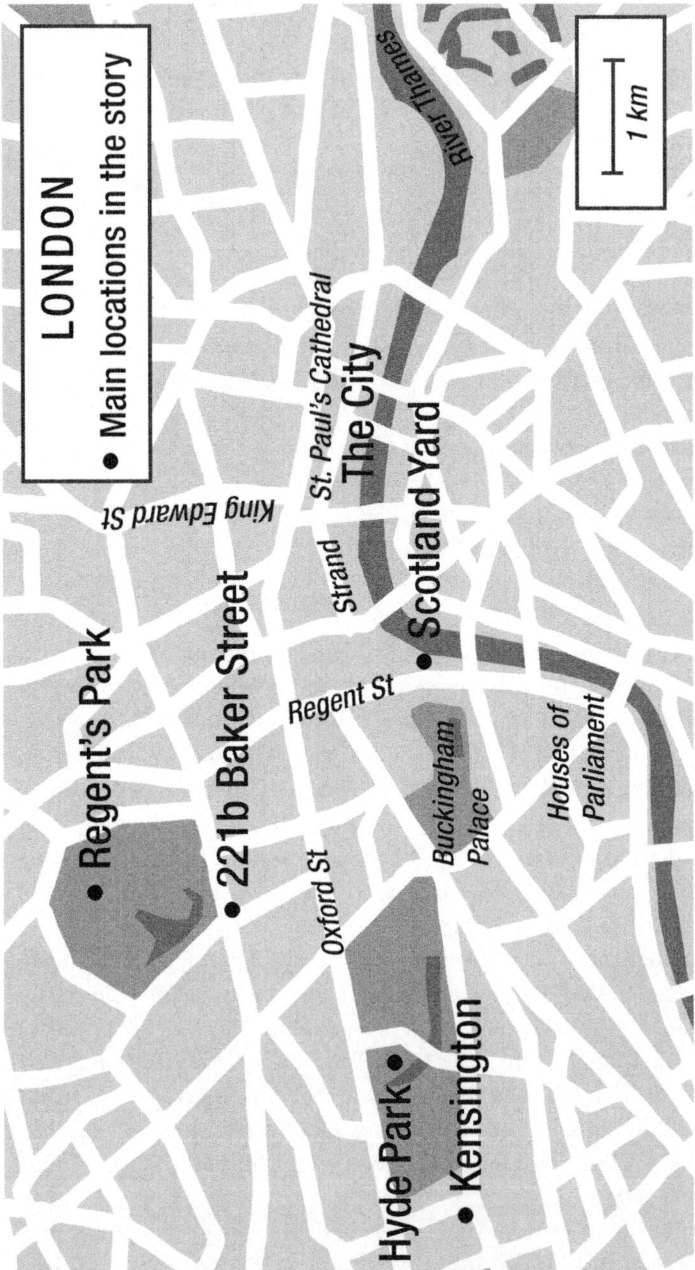
LONDON
• Main locations in the story
• Regent's Park
• 221b Baker Street
King Edward St
St. Paul's Cathedral
The City
Strand
• Scotland Yard
River Thames
1 km
Regent St
Oxford St
Buckingham Palace
Houses of Parliament
Hyde Park •
• Kensington

# THE RED-HEADED LEAGUE

I had called upon my friend, Mr. Sherlock Holmes, one day in the autumn of last year[1] and found him in deep conversation with a very stout, florid-faced,[2] elderly gentleman with fiery red hair. With an apology for my intrusion, I was about to withdraw when Holmes pulled me abruptly into the room and closed the door behind me.

"You could not possibly have come at a better time, my dear Watson," he said cordially.[3]

"I was afraid that you were engaged."

"So I am. Very much so."

"Then I can wait in the next room."

"Not at all. This gentleman, Mr. Wilson, has been my partner and helper in many of my most successful cases, and I have no doubt that he will be of the utmost use to me in yours also."

The stout gentleman half rose from his chair and gave a bob of greeting, with a quick little questioning glance from his small fat-encircled eyes.

"Try the settee,[4]" said Holmes, relapsing into his armchair and putting his fingertips together, as was his custom when in judicial moods. "I know, my dear Watson, that you share my love of all that is bizarre and outside the conventions and humdrum routine of everyday life. You have shown your relish for it by the enthusiasm which has prompted you to chronicle,[5] and, if you will excuse my saying so, somewhat to embellish[6] so many of my own little adventures."

---

1 1891.

2 Having a ruddy, flushed or highly coloured complexion.

3 Heart-felt, sincere.

4 An upholstered chair with space for more than one person. Nowadays, many British people call this a sofa and think that this word is somehow more refined than the more "common" settee. However, at the time of writing it was probably the case that a sofa had arms and a settee did not.

5 To write down for publication.

6 To add interest to a story.

"Your cases have indeed been of the greatest interest to me," I observed.

"You will remember that I remarked the other day, just before we went into the very simple problem presented by Miss Mary Sutherland,[7] that for strange effects and extraordinary combinations we must go to life itself, which is always far more daring than any effort of the imagination."

"A proposition which I took the liberty of doubting."

"You did, Doctor, but none the less you must come round to my view, for otherwise I shall keep on piling fact upon fact on you until your reason breaks down under them and acknowledges me to be right. Now, Mr. Jabez Wilson here has been good enough to call upon me this morning, and to begin a narrative which promises to be one of the most singular which I have listened to for some time. You have heard me remark that the strangest and most unique things are very often connected not with the larger but with the smaller crimes, and occasionally, indeed, where there is room for doubt whether any positive crime has been committed. As far as I have heard, it is impossible for me to say whether the present case is an instance of crime or not, but the course of events is certainly among the most singular that I have ever listened to. Perhaps, Mr. Wilson, you would have the great kindness to recommence your narrative. I ask you not merely because my friend Dr. Watson has not heard the opening part but also because the peculiar nature of the story makes me anxious to have every possible detail from your lips. As a rule, when I have heard some slight indication of the course of events, I am able to guide myself by the thousands of other similar cases which occur to my memory. In the present

7 Miss Sutherland appears in the next story in the series (*A Case of Identity*). This was originally published in *The Strand Magazine* a month after the present story. Perhaps the publisher decided to change the order of publication.

MR. JABEZ WILSON.

instance I am forced to admit that the facts are, to the best of my belief, unique."

The portly client puffed out his chest with an appearance of some little pride and pulled a dirty and wrinkled newspaper from the inside pocket of his greatcoat. As he glanced down the advertisement column, with his head thrust forward and the paper flattened out upon his knee, I took a good look at the man and endeavoured, after the fashion of my companion, to read the indications which might be presented by his dress or appearance.

I did not gain very much, however, by my inspection. Our visitor bore every mark of being an average commonplace British tradesman, obese, pompous, and slow. He wore rather baggy grey shepherd's check trousers,[8] a not over-clean black frock-coat,[9] unbuttoned in the front, and a drab waistcoat with a heavy brassy albert chain,[10] and a square pierced bit of metal dangling down as an ornament. A frayed top-hat and a faded brown overcoat with a wrinkled velvet collar lay upon a chair beside him. Altogether, look as I would, there was nothing remarkable about the man save his blazing red head, and the expression of extreme chagrin[11] and discontent upon his features.

Sherlock Holmes's quick eye took in my occupation, and he shook his head with a smile as he noticed my questioning glances. "Beyond the obvious facts that he has at some time done manual labour, that he takes snuff,[12] that he is a Freemason,[13] that he has been in China, and that he has done a considerable amount of writing lately, I can deduce nothing else."

Mr. Jabez Wilson started up in his chair, with his forefinger upon the paper, but his eyes upon my companion.

"How, in the name of good-fortune, did you know all that, Mr. Holmes?" he asked. "How did you know, for example, that I did manual labour. It's as true as gospel, for I began as a ship's carpenter."

"Your hands, my dear sir. Your right hand is quite a size larger than your left. You have worked with it, and the muscles are more developed."

"Well, the snuff, then, and the Freemasonry?"

---

8 A small black and white plaid.

9 A long-skirted jacket.

10 A watch-chain that attached to a buttonhole. It was made popular by Queen Victoria's husband, Prince Albert, who died in 1861.

11 Annoyance.

12 A powdered tobacco taken by sniffing up the nostrils.

13 A member of a secretive group of men giving each other help and fellowship.

"I won't insult your intelligence by telling you how I read that, especially as, rather against the strict rules of your order, you use an arc-and-compass breastpin."[14]

"Ah, of course, I forgot that. But the writing?"

"What else can be indicated by that right cuff so very shiny for five inches, and the left one with the smooth patch near the elbow where you rest it upon the desk?"

"Well, but China?"

"The fish that you have tattooed immediately above your right wrist could only have been done in China. I have made a small study of tattoo marks and have even contributed to the literature of the subject. That trick of staining the fishes' scales of a delicate pink is quite peculiar to China. When, in addition, I see a Chinese coin[15] hanging from your watch-chain, the matter becomes even more simple."

Mr. Jabez Wilson laughed heavily. "Well, I never!" said he. "I thought at first that you had done something clever, but I see that there was nothing in it after all."

"I begin to think, Watson," said Holmes, "that I make a mistake in explaining. '*Omne ignotum pro magnifico*,'[16] you know, and my poor little reputation, such as it is, will suffer shipwreck if I am so candid.[17] Can you not find the advertisement, Mr. Wilson?"

"Yes, I have got it now," he answered with his thick red finger planted halfway down the column. "Here it is. This is what began it all. You just read it for yourself, sir."

I took the paper from him and read as follows:

---

14 An arc and compass together is the symbol of Freemasonry. Here Mr. Wilson wore it as a badge rather against the secretive nature of the society.

15 Some Chinese coins had a central hole.

16 From the Latin for "Everything unknown appears magnificent." Probably from Tacitus (56–117AD) who was a Roman senator and historian. Watson would probably have understood this, but Mr. Wilson would probably not have comprehended since he did not have the benefit of a classical education as he was an "average commonplace British tradesman".

17 Open, honest.

"TO THE RED-HEADED LEAGUE: On account of the bequest of the late Ezekiah Hopkins, of Lebanon,[18] Pennsylvania, U.S.A., there is now another vacancy open which entitles a member of the League to a salary of £4 a week for purely nominal services. All red-headed men who are sound in body and mind and above the age of twenty-one years, are eligible. Apply in person on Monday, at eleven o'clock, to Duncan Ross, at the offices of the League, 7 Pope's Court, Fleet Street."[19]

"What on earth does this mean?" I ejaculated[20] after I had twice read over the extraordinary announcement.

Holmes chuckled and wriggled in his chair, as was his habit when in high spirits. "It is a little off the beaten track,[21] isn't it?" said he. "And now, Mr. Wilson, off you go at scratch and tell us all about yourself, your household, and the effect which this advertisement had upon your fortunes. You will first make a note, Doctor, of the paper and the date."

"It is *The Morning Chronicle*[22] of April 27, 1890.[23] Just two months ago."

"Very good. Now, Mr. Wilson?"

"Well, it is just as I have been telling you, Mr. Sherlock Holmes," said Jabez Wilson, mopping his forehead; "I have

18 It was named Lebanon in 1885, but prior to that date it was know as Steitztown after its founder George Steitz in 1740.

19 Pope's Court does not exist. Fleet Street was named after the River Fleet which runs beneath it. The street connects the commercial part of London (the City) in the east to the political centre (Westminster) in the west.

20 Speak suddenly.

21 Off the beaten track is still a common expression meaning to be away from the ordinary or usual.

22 A London newspaper first published in 1769 until 1862. It is not clear why a paper that was no longer published was used in the story.

23 This was a Sunday. It is strange as the *Morning Chronicle* was not published on a Sunday.

WHAT ON EARTH DOES THIS MEAN?

a small pawnbroker's[24] business at Coburg Square,[25] near the City.[26] It's not a very large affair, and of late years it has not done more than just give me a living. I used to be able to keep two assistants, but now I only keep one; and I would have a

24 A pawnbroker is someone who lends money on the security of personal property.

25 Later in the story also called Saxe-Coburg Square; it is probably a made up place as it no longer exists.

26 The City of London (with a capital C) is a separate district within London. It is also the financial centre of London.

job to pay him but that he is willing to come for half wages so as to learn the business."

"What is the name of this obliging youth?" asked Sherlock Holmes.

"His name is Vincent Spaulding, and he's not such a youth, either. It's hard to say his age. I should not wish a smarter assistant, Mr. Holmes; and I know very well that he could better himself and earn twice what I am able to give him. But, after all, if he is satisfied, why should I put ideas in his head?"

"Why, indeed? You seem most fortunate in having an employ who comes under the full market price. It is not a common experience among employers in this age. I don't know that your assistant is not as remarkable as your advertisement."

"Oh, he has his faults, too," said Mr. Wilson. "Never was such a fellow for photography. Snapping away with a camera when he ought to be improving his mind, and then diving down into the cellar like a rabbit into its hole to develop his pictures.[27] That is his main fault, but on the whole he's a good worker. There's no vice[28] in him."

"He is still with you, I presume?"

"Yes, sir. He and a girl of fourteen,[29] who does a bit of simple cooking and keeps the place clean – that's all I have in the house, for I am a widower and never had any family. We live very quietly, sir, the three of us; and we keep a roof over our heads and pay our debts, if we do nothing more.

---

27 Developing a photographic negative needed to be done in complete darkness. Kodak's popular Box Brownie camera brought photography to the masses and was introduced in 1888.

28 Evil.

29 Child labour was becoming less common at this time, but it was estimated that there were 500 girls below 15 years of age working in mines and 82,600 in textiles businesses. There must have been many more in domestic service.

"The first thing that put us out was that advertisement. Spaulding, he came down into the office just this day eight weeks, with this very paper in his hand, and he says:

" 'I wish to the Lord, Mr. Wilson, that I was a red-headed man.'

" 'Why that?' I asks.

" 'Why,' says he, 'here's another vacancy on the League of the Red-Headed Men. It's worth quite a little fortune to any man who gets it, and I understand that there are more vacancies than there are men, so that the trustees are at their wits' end what to do with the money. If my hair would only change colour, here's a nice little crib[30] all ready for me to step into.'

" 'Why, what is it, then?' I asked. You see, Mr. Holmes, I am a very stay-at-home man, and as my business came to me instead of my having to go to it, I was often weeks on end without putting my foot over the door-mat. In that way I didn't know much of what was going on outside, and I was always glad of a bit of news.

" 'Have you never heard of the League of the Red-Headed Men?' he asked with his eyes open.

" 'Never.'

" 'Why, I wonder at that, for you are eligible yourself for one of the vacancies.'

" 'And what are they worth?' I asked.

" 'Oh, merely a couple of hundred a year, but the work is slight, and it need not interfere very much with one's other occupations.'

"Well, you can easily think that that made me prick up my ears, for the business has not been over good for some years, and an extra couple of hundred would have been very handy.

" 'Tell me all about it,' said I.

---

30 Slang for a house or dwelling, or in this sense, position. The word dropped out of use but has recently had a comeback as a slang word, particularly in the USA, for a living place.

" 'Well,' said he, showing me the advertisement, 'you can see for yourself that the League has a vacancy, and there is the address where you should apply for particulars. As far as I can make out, the League was founded by an American millionaire, Ezekiah Hopkins, who was very peculiar in his ways. He was himself red-headed, and he had a great sympathy for all red-headed men; so, when he died, it was found that he had left his enormous fortune in the hands of trustees, with instructions to apply the interest to the providing of easy berths to men whose hair is of that colour. From all I hear it is splendid pay and very little to do.'

" 'But,' said I, 'there would be millions of red-headed men who would apply.'

THE LEAGUE HAS A VACANCY.

"'Not so many as you might think,' he answered. 'You see it is really confined to Londoners, and to grown men. This American had started from London when he was young, and he wanted to do the old town a good turn. Then, again, I have heard it is no use your applying if your hair is light red, or dark red, or anything but real bright, blazing, fiery red. Now, if you cared to apply, Mr. Wilson, you would just walk in; but perhaps it would hardly be worth your while to put yourself out of the way for the sake of a few hundred pounds.'

"Now, it is a fact, gentlemen, as you may see for yourselves, that my hair is of a very full and rich tint, so that it seemed to me that if there was to be any competition in the matter I stood as good a chance as any man that I had ever met. Vincent Spaulding seemed to know so much about it that I thought he might prove useful, so I just ordered him to put up the shutters for the day[31] and to come right away with me. He was very willing to have a holiday, so we shut the business up and started off for the address that was given us in the advertisement.

"I never hope to see such a sight as that again, Mr. Holmes. From north, south, east, and west every man who had a shade of red in his hair had tramped into the city to answer the advertisement. Fleet Street was choked with red-headed folk, and Pope's Court looked like a coster's[32] orange barrow. I should not have thought there were so many in the whole country as were brought together by that single advertisement. Every shade of colour they were – straw, lemon, orange, brick, Irish-setter, liver, clay; but, as Spaulding said, there were not many who had the real vivid flame-coloured tint. When I saw how many were waiting, I would have given it up in despair; but Spaulding would not hear of it. How he did it I

---

31 Although this was probably in the literal sense, the expression is still sometimes used to indicate closing up.

32 Shortened version of costermonger: someone who sold fruit or vegetables from a barrow in the street.

could not imagine, but he pushed and pulled and butted until he got me through the crowd, and right up to the steps which led to the office. There was a double stream upon the stair, some going up in hope, and some coming back dejected; but we wedged in as well as we could and soon found ourselves in the office."

"Your experience has been a most entertaining one," remarked Holmes as his client paused and refreshed his memory with a huge pinch of snuff. "Pray continue your very interesting statement."

"There was nothing in the office but a couple of wooden chairs and a deal table,[33] behind which sat a small man with a head that was even redder than mine. He said a few words to each candidate as he came up, and then he always managed to find some fault in them which would disqualify them. Getting a vacancy did not seem to be such a very easy matter, after all. However, when our turn came the little man was much more favourable to me than to any of the others, and he closed the door as we entered, so that he might have a private word with us.

" 'This is Mr. Jabez Wilson,' said my assistant, 'and he is willing to fill a vacancy in the League.'

" 'And he is admirably suited for it,' the other answered. 'He has every requirement. I cannot recall when I have seen anything so fine.' He took a step backward, cocked his head on one side, and gazed at my hair until I felt quite bashful. Then suddenly he plunged forward, wrung my hand, and congratulated me warmly on my success.

" 'It would be injustice to hesitate,' said he. 'You will, however, I am sure, excuse me for taking an obvious precaution.' With that he seized my hair in both his hands, and tugged until I yelled with the pain. 'There is water in your eyes,' said he as he released me. 'I perceive that all is as it should be.

33 A table made from sawn planks of fir or pine.

HE CONGRATULATED ME WARMLY.

But we have to be careful, for we have twice been deceived by wigs and once by paint. I could tell you tales of cobbler's wax[34] which would disgust you with human nature.' He stepped over to the window and shouted through it at the top of his voice that the vacancy was filled. A groan of disappointment came up from below, and the folk all trooped away in different directions until there was not a red-head to be seen except my own and that of the manager.

34 Resin used to coat thread.

" 'My name,' said he, 'is Mr. Duncan Ross, and I am myself one of the pensioners upon the fund left by our noble benefactor. Are you a married man, Mr. Wilson? Have you a family?'

"I answered that I had not.

"His face fell immediately.

" 'Dear me!' he said gravely, 'that is very serious indeed! I am sorry to hear you say that. The fund was, of course, for the propagation and spread of the red-heads as well as for their maintenance. It is exceedingly unfortunate that you should be a bachelor.'

"My face lengthened at this, Mr. Holmes, for I thought that I was not to have the vacancy after all; but after thinking it over for a few minutes he said that it would be all right.

" 'In the case of another,' said he, 'the objection might be fatal, but we must stretch a point in favour of a man with such a head of hair as yours. When shall you be able to enter upon your new duties?'

" 'Well, it is a little awkward, for I have a business already,' said I.

" 'Oh, never mind about that, Mr. Wilson!' said Vincent Spaulding. 'I should be able to look after that for you.'

" 'What would be the hours?' I asked.

" 'Ten to two.'

"Now a pawnbroker's business is mostly done of an evening, Mr. Holmes, especially Thursday and Friday evening, which is just before pay-day; so it would suit me very well to earn a little in the mornings. Besides, I knew that my assistant was a good man, and that he would see to anything that turned up.

" 'That would suit me very well,' said I. 'And the pay?'

" 'Is £4 a week.'[35]

" 'And the work?'

35 About £240 in today's money and about the same as the wage for a well-paid full-time clerk.

" 'Is purely nominal.'

" 'What do you call purely nominal?'

" 'Well, you have to be in the office, or at least in the building, the whole time. If you leave, you forfeit your whole position forever. The will is very clear upon that point. You don't comply with the conditions if you budge from the office during that time.'

" 'It's only four hours a day, and I should not think of leaving,' said I.

" 'No excuse will avail,' said Mr. Duncan Ross; 'neither sickness nor business nor anything else. There you must stay, or you lose your billet.'[36]

" 'And the work?'

" 'Is to copy out the *Encyclopaedia Britannica*.[37] There is the first volume of it in that press.[38] You must find your own ink, pens, and blotting-paper,[39] but we provide this table and chair. Will you be ready tomorrow?'

" 'Certainly,' I answered.

" 'Then, goodbye, Mr. Jabez Wilson, and let me congratulate you once more on the important position which you have been fortunate enough to gain.' He bowed me out of the room and I went home with my assistant, hardly knowing what to say or do, I was so pleased at my own good fortune.

"Well, I thought over the matter all day, and by evening I was in low spirits again; for I had quite persuaded myself that the whole affair must be some great hoax or fraud, though what its object might be I could not imagine. It seemed altogether past belief that anyone could make such a will, or that they would pay such a sum for doing anything so simple as copying out the *Encyclopaedia Britannica*. Vincent

36 Another term for a job or situation.

37 A multi-volume encyclopedia.

38 In this sense, a press is a kind of bookcase.

39 This would have been used to soak up the excess liquid ink from pens of the time.

Spaulding did what he could to cheer me up, but by bedtime I had reasoned myself out of the whole thing. However, in the morning I determined to have a look at it anyhow, so I bought a penny bottle of ink, and with a quill-pen,[40] and seven sheets of foolscap paper,[41] I started off for Pope's Court.

"Well, to my surprise and delight, everything was as right as possible. The table was set out ready for me, and Mr. Duncan Ross was there to see that I got fairly to work. He started me off upon the letter A, and then he left me; but he would drop in from time to time to see that all was right with me. At two o'clock he bade me good-day, complimented me upon the amount that I had written, and locked the door of the office after me.

"This went on day after day, Mr. Holmes, and on Saturday the manager came in and planked down four golden sovereigns[42] for my week's work. It was the same next week, and the same the week after. Every morning I was there at ten, and every afternoon I left at two. By degrees Mr. Duncan Ross took to coming in only once of a morning, and then, after a time, he did not come in at all. Still, of course, I never dared to leave the room for an instant, for I was not sure when he might come, and the billet was such a good one, and suited me so well, that I would not risk the loss of it.

"Eight weeks passed away like this, and I had written about Abbots and Archery and Armour and Architecture and Attica, and hoped with diligence that I might get on to the B's before very long. It cost me something in foolscap, and I had pretty nearly filled a shelf with my writings. And then suddenly the whole business came to an end."

"To an end?"

---

40 A pen made from a bird's feather.

41 This indicates the size of the sheet of paper. It is roughly the same size as A4 or letter paper.

42 A sovereign was gold coin with a value of £1.

"Yes, sir. And no later than this morning. I went to my work as usual at ten o'clock, but the door was shut and locked, with a little square of cardboard hammered on to the middle of the panel with a tack. Here it is, and you can read for yourself."

He held up a piece of white cardboard about the size of a sheet of notepaper. It read in this fashion:

THE RED-HEADED LEAGUE
IS
DISSOLVED.
October 9, 1890.

THE DOOR WAS SHUT AND LOCKED.

Sherlock Holmes and I surveyed this curt announcement and the rueful face behind it, until the comical side of the affair so completely overtopped every other consideration that we both burst out into a roar of laughter.

"I cannot see that there is anything very funny," cried our client, flushing up to the roots of his flaming head. "If you can do nothing better than laugh at me, I can go elsewhere."

"No, no," cried Holmes, shoving him back into the chair from which he had half risen. "I really wouldn't miss your case for the world. It is most refreshingly unusual. But there is, if you will excuse my saying so, something just a little funny about it. Pray what steps did you take when you found the card upon the door?"

"I was staggered, sir. I did not know what to do. Then I called at the offices round, but none of them seemed to know anything about it. Finally, I went to the landlord,[43] who is an accountant living on the ground floor, and I asked him if he could tell me what had become of the Red-Headed League. He said that he had never heard of any such body. Then I asked him who Mr. Duncan Ross was. He answered that the name was new to him.

" 'Well,' said I, 'the gentleman at No. 4.'

" 'What, the red-headed man?'

" 'Yes.'

" 'Oh,' said he, 'his name was William Morris. He was a solicitor[44] and was using my room as a temporary convenience until his new premises were ready. He moved out yesterday.'

" 'Where could I find him?'

" 'Oh, at his new offices. He did tell me the address. Yes, 17 King Edward Street, near St. Paul's.'[45]

43 The owner of the building.

44 A type of lawyer who does not present cases in court.

45 There is such a street near St. Paul's Cathedral.

"I started off, Mr. Holmes, but when I got to that address it was a manufactory[46] of artificial knee-caps, and no one in it had ever heard of either Mr. William Morris or Mr. Duncan Ross."

"And what did you do then?" asked Holmes.

"I went home to Saxe-Coburg Square,[47] and I took the advice of my assistant. But he could not help me in any way. He could only say that if I waited I should hear by post. But that was not quite good enough, Mr. Holmes. I did not wish to lose such a place without a struggle, so, as I had heard that you were good enough to give advice to poor folk who were in need of it, I came right away to you."

"And you did very wisely," said Holmes. "Your case is an exceedingly remarkable one, and I shall be happy to look into it. From what you have told me I think that it is possible that graver issues hang from it than might at first sight appear."

"Grave enough!" said Mr. Jabez Wilson. "Why, I have lost £4 a week."

"As far as you are personally concerned," remarked Holmes, "I do not see that you have any grievance against this extraordinary league. On the contrary, you are, as I understand, richer by some £30, to say nothing of the minute knowledge which you have gained on every subject which comes under the letter A. You have lost nothing by them."

"No, sir. But I want to find out about them, and who they are, and what their object was in playing this prank – if it was a prank – upon me. It was a pretty expensive joke for them, for it cost them two and thirty pounds."

"We shall endeavour to clear up these points for you. And, first, one or two questions, Mr. Wilson. This assistant of yours who first called your attention to the advertisement – how long had he been with you?"

---

46 Now more commonly called a factory.

47 Earlier Mr. Wilson referred to his address as Coburg Square.

"About a month then."

"How did he come?"

"In answer to an advertisement."

"Was he the only applicant?"

"No, I had a dozen."

"Why did you pick him?"

"Because he was handy and would come cheap."

"At half wages, in fact."

"Yes."

"What is he like, this Vincent Spaulding?"

"Small, stout-built, very quick in his ways, no hair on his face, though he's not short of thirty. Has a white splash of acid upon his forehead."

Holmes sat up in his chair in considerable excitement. "I thought as much," said he. "Have you ever observed that his ears are pierced for earrings?"

"Yes, sir. He told me that a gypsy had done it for him when he was a lad."

"Hum!" said Holmes, sinking back in deep thought. "He is still with you?"

"Oh, yes, sir; I have only just left him."

"And has your business been attended to in your absence?"

"Nothing to complain of, sir. There's never very much to do of a morning."

"That will do, Mr. Wilson. I shall be happy

to give you an opinion upon the subject in the course of a day or two. Today is Saturday, and I hope that by Monday we may come to a conclusion."

"Well, Watson," said Holmes when our visitor had left us, "what do you make of it all?"

"I make nothing of it," I answered frankly. "It is a most mysterious business."

"As a rule," said Holmes, "the more bizarre a thing is the less mysterious it proves to be. It is your commonplace, featureless crimes which are really puzzling, just as a commonplace face is the most difficult to identify. But I must be prompt over this matter."

"What are you going to do, then?" I asked.

"To smoke," he answered. "It is quite a three-pipe problem,[48] and I beg that you won't speak to me for fifty minutes." He curled himself up in his chair, with his thin knees drawn up to his hawk-like nose, and there he sat with his eyes closed and his black clay pipe thrusting out like the bill of some strange bird. I had come to the conclusion that he had dropped asleep, and indeed was nodding myself, when he suddenly sprang out of his chair with the gesture of a man who has made up his mind and put his pipe down upon the mantelpiece.

"Sarasate[49] plays at the St. James's Hall[50] this afternoon," he remarked. "What do you think, Watson? Could your patients spare you for a few hours?"

"I have nothing to do today. My practice is never very absorbing."

"Then put on your hat and come. I am going through the City first, and we can have some lunch on the way. I observe

48 Holmes needs enough time to smoke three pipes in order to think through the problem.

49 Pablo de Sarasate (1844–1908) was a popular Spanish violinist and composer who had played in London (but in 1874, six years before the setting of this story).

50 This was a concert hall opened in 1858 situated between Piccadilly and Regent Street.

that there is a good deal of German music on the programme, which is rather more to my taste than Italian or French. It is introspective, and I want to introspect. Come along!"

We travelled by the Underground[51] as far as Aldersgate;[52] and a short walk took us to Saxe-Coburg Square, the scene of the singular story which we had listened to in the morning. It was a poky, little, shabby-genteel[53] place, where four lines of dingy two-storied brick houses looked out into a small railed-in enclosure, where a lawn of weedy grass and a few clumps of faded laurel bushes made a hard fight against a smoke-laden and uncongenial atmosphere. Three gilt balls[54] and a brown board with "JABEZ WILSON" in white letters, upon a corner house, announced the place where our red-headed client carried on his business. Sherlock Holmes stopped in front of it with his head on one side and looked it all over, with his eyes shining brightly between puckered lids. Then he walked slowly up the street, and then down again to the corner, still looking keenly at the houses. Finally he returned to the pawnbroker's, and, having thumped vigorously upon the pavement with his stick two or three times, he went up to the door and knocked. It was instantly opened by a bright-looking, clean-shaven young fellow, who asked him to step in.

"Thank you," said Holmes, "I only wished to ask you how you would go from here to the Strand."[55]

"Third right, fourth left," answered the assistant promptly, closing the door.

"Smart fellow, that," observed Holmes as we walked away. "He is, in my judgement, the fourth smartest man in London,

---

51 More commonly called the tube nowadays. This is the only mention of Holmes ever using this new mass-transit railway.

52 Renamed Barbican station in 1968.

53 Keeps some dignity despite shabbiness.

54 The three gold-coloured balls were the symbol of a pawnbroker's business.

55 A major road in central London. It contained the offices of *The Strand Magazine*. A strand is another name for a shore or river-bank and the road would have originally been close to the River Thames.

THE DOOR WAS INSTANTLY OPENED.

and for daring I am not sure that he has not a claim to be third. I have known something of him before."

"Evidently," said I, "Mr. Wilson's assistant counts for a good deal in this mystery of the Red-Headed League. I am sure that you inquired your way merely in order that you might see him."

"Not him."

"What then?"

"The knees of his trousers."

"And what did you see?"

"What I expected to see."

"Why did you beat the pavement?"

"My dear doctor, this is a time for observation, not for talk. We are spies in an enemy's country. We know something of Saxe-Coburg Square. Let us now explore the parts which lie behind it."

The road in which we found ourselves as we turned round the corner from the retired Saxe-Coburg Square presented as great a contrast to it as the front of a picture does to the back. It was one of the main arteries which conveyed the traffic of the City to the north and west. The roadway was blocked with the immense stream of commerce flowing in a double tide inward and outward, while the footpaths were black with the hurrying swarm of pedestrians. It was difficult to realize as we looked at the line of fine shops and stately business premises that they really abutted on the other side upon the faded and stagnant square which we had just quitted.

"Let me see," said Holmes, standing at the corner and glancing along the line, "I should like just to remember the order of the houses here. It is a hobby of mine to have an exact knowledge of London. There is Mortimer's, the tobacconist, the little newspaper shop, the Coburg branch of the City and Suburban Bank, the vegetarian restaurant, and McFarlane's carriage-building depot. That carries us right on to the other block. And now, Doctor, we've done our work, so it's time we had some play. A sandwich and a cup of coffee, and then off to violin-land, where all is sweetness and delicacy and harmony, and there are no red-headed clients to vex[56] us with their conundrums."[57]

56 To annoy.

57 Problems.

My friend was an enthusiastic musician, being himself not only a very capable performer but a composer of no ordinary merit. All the afternoon he sat in the stalls wrapped in the most perfect happiness, gently waving his long, thin fingers in time to the music, while his gently smiling face and his languid, dreamy eyes were as unlike those of Holmes the sleuth-hound, Holmes the relentless, keen-witted, ready-handed criminal agent, as it was possible to conceive. In his singular character the dual nature alternately asserted itself, and his extreme exactness and astuteness represented, as I have often thought, the reaction against the poetic and contemplative mood which occasionally predominated in him. The swing of his nature took him from extreme languor[58] to devouring energy; and, as I knew well, he was never so truly formidable as when, for days on end, he had been lounging in his armchair amid his improvisations and his black-letter editions.[59] Then it was that the lust of the chase[60] would suddenly come upon him, and that his brilliant reasoning power would rise to the level of intuition, until those who were unacquainted with his methods would look askance at him as on a man whose knowledge was not that of other mortals. When I saw him that afternoon so enwrapped in the music at St. James's Hall I felt that an evil time might be coming upon those whom he had set himself to hunt down.

"You want to go home, no doubt, Doctor," he remarked as we emerged.[61]

"Yes, it would be as well."

"And I have some business to do which will take some hours. This business at Coburg Square is serious."

---

58 Idleness.

59 These were ancient books, so-called after the heavy style of type used.

60 "Lust of the chase" is probably a hunting metaphor indicating the excitement of the case to Holmes. Holmes is often pictured wearing a deerstalker hat and he uses a riding crop, but there is no mention of him actually hunting.

61 Watson was married and had a medical practice to take care of.

ALL AFTERNOON HE SAT IN THE STALLS.

"Why serious?"

"A considerable crime is in contemplation. I have every reason to believe that we shall be in time to stop it. But today being Saturday rather complicates matters. I shall want your help tonight."

"At what time?"

"Ten will be early enough."

"I shall be at Baker Street at ten."[62]

"Very well. And, I say, Doctor, there may be some little danger, so kindly put your army revolver[63] in your pocket." He waved his hand, turned on his heel, and disappeared in an instant among the crowd.

I trust that I am not more dense than my neighbours, but I was always oppressed with a sense of my own stupidity in my dealings with Sherlock Holmes. Here I had heard what he had heard, I had seen what he had seen, and yet from his words it was evident that he saw clearly not only what had happened but what was about to happen, while to me the whole business was still confused and grotesque.[64] As I drove home to my house in Kensington[65] I thought over it all, from the extraordinary story of the red-headed copier of the *Encyclopaedia* down to the visit to Saxe-Coburg Square, and the ominous words with which he had parted from me. What was this nocturnal[66] expedition, and why should I go armed? Where were we going, and what were we to do? I had the hint

---

62 Baker Street was a residential area in central London. The houses were terraced – that is built with shared walls – and made of brick. The address is 221b Baker Street. This didn't exist when the story was written, but the address was assigned in 1990 and houses the Sherlock Holmes Museum. There is no 221a: the "b" represents *bis*, the Latin for "twice". Holmes lived in a rented apartment attached or converted from 221. This would probably have been owned by Mrs. Hudson, Holmes's long-suffering landlady and cook.

63 This was very probably a six-shot Webley & Scott revolver.

64 Unnatural.

65 An affluent district in west London, a short distance from Baker Street.

66 Night-time.

from Holmes that this smooth-faced pawnbroker's assistant was a formidable man – a man who might play a deep game. I tried to puzzle it out, but gave it up in despair and set the matter aside until night should bring an explanation.

It was a quarter-past nine when I started from home and made my way across the Park,[67] and so through Oxford Street to Baker Street. Two hansoms[68] were standing at the door, and as I entered the passage I heard the sound of voices from above. On entering his room, I found Holmes in animated conversation with two men, one of whom I recognized as Peter Jones, the official police agent, while the other was a long, thin, sad-faced man, with a very shiny hat and oppressively respectable frock-coat.

"Ha! Our party is complete," said Holmes, buttoning up his pea-jacket[69] and taking his heavy hunting crop from the rack. "Watson, I think you know Mr. Jones, of Scotland Yard?[70] Let me introduce you to Mr. Merryweather, who is to be our companion in tonight's adventure."

"We're hunting in couples again, Doctor, you see," said Jones in his consequential way. "Our friend here is a wonderful man for starting a chase. All he wants is an old dog to help him to do the running down."

"I hope a wild goose[71] may not prove to be the end of our chase," observed Mr. Merryweather gloomily.

"You may place considerable confidence in Mr. Holmes, sir," said the police agent loftily. "He has his own little methods, which are, if he won't mind my saying so, just a little too theoretical and fantastic, but he has the makings of a detective in him. It is not too much to say that once or twice, as in

67 Probably Hyde Park.

68 In full, a hansom cab was a two-wheeled carriage pulled by a single horse.

69 A thigh-length, heavy, dark-coloured woollen coat.

70 Scotland Yard was the headquarters of London's police. The present headquarters is at New Scotland Yard in a different district to the original site.

71 From "a wild-goose chase": indicating a fruitless and pointless exercise.

that business of the Sholto murder and the Agra treasure,[72] he has been more nearly correct than the official force."

"Oh, if you say so, Mr. Jones, it is all right," said the stranger with deference. "Still, I confess that I miss my rubber.[73] It is the first Saturday night for seven-and-twenty[74] years that I have not had my rubber."

"I think you will find," said Sherlock Holmes, "that you will play for a higher stake tonight than you have ever done yet, and that the play will be more exciting. For you, Mr. Merryweather, the stake will be some £30,000;[75] and for you, Jones, it will be the man upon whom you wish to lay your hands."

"John Clay, the murderer, thief, smasher,[76] and forger. He's a young man, Mr. Merryweather, but he is at the head of his profession, and I would rather have my bracelets[77] on him than on any criminal in London. He's a remarkable man, is young John Clay. His grandfather was a royal duke, and he himself has been to Eton and Oxford.[78] His brain is as cunning as his fingers, and though we meet signs of him at every turn, we never know where to find the man himself. He'll crack a crib in Scotland one week, and be raising money to build an orphanage in Cornwall the next. I've been on his track for years and have never set eyes on him yet."

"I hope that I may have the pleasure of introducing you tonight. I've had one or two little turns also with Mr. John

72 Both of these cases are covered in the novel *The Sign of Four*, Conan Doyle's second Holmes novel, published in 1890.

73 A rubber is a hand of cards in a playing-card game called bridge.

74 Nowadays, this is an unusual way of expressing "twenty-seven", although some older people still do, particularly for numbers in the twenties.

75 The equivalent of £1.8 million in today's money.

76 Nowadays, this is used for a beautiful object or person: "look at this smasher". In this archaic sense it someone who passes on counterfeit coins.

77 Slang for handcuffs.

78 This would show a rich or aristocratic background. Eton is still thought of as one of the most prestigious schools in the UK, and Oxford one of its most renowned universities.

Clay, and I agree with you that he is at the head of his profession. It is past ten, however, and quite time that we started. If you two will take the first hansom, Watson and I will follow in the second."

Sherlock Holmes was not very communicative during the long drive and lay back in the cab humming the tunes which he had heard in the afternoon. We rattled through an endless labyrinth of gas-lit streets until we emerged into Farrington Street.[79]

"We are close there now," my friend remarked. "This fellow Merryweather is a bank director, and personally interested in the matter. I thought it as well to have Jones with us also. He is not a bad fellow, though an absolute imbecile in his profession. He has one positive virtue. He is as brave as a bulldog and as tenacious as a lobster if he gets his claws upon anyone. Here we are, and they are waiting for us."

We had reached the same crowded thoroughfare in which we had found ourselves in the morning. Our cabs were dismissed, and, following the guidance of Mr. Merryweather, we passed down a narrow passage and through a side door, which he opened for us. Within there was a small corridor, which ended in a very massive iron gate. This also was opened, and led down a flight of winding stone steps, which terminated at another formidable gate. Mr. Merryweather stopped to light a lantern, and then conducted us down a dark, earth-smelling passage, and so, after opening a third door, into a huge vault or cellar, which was piled all round with crates and massive boxes.

"You are not very vulnerable from above," Holmes remarked as he held up the lantern and gazed about him.

"Nor from below," said Mr. Merryweather, striking his stick upon the flags[80] which lined the floor. "Why, dear me, it sounds quite hollow!" he remarked, looking up in surprise.

79 Presumably this is a made-up street name as it does not exist now.
80 Flagstones: large, flat stones for flooring or similar purposes.

MR. MERRYWEATHER STOPPED TO LIGHT A LANTERN.

"I must really ask you to be a little more quiet!" said Holmes severely. "You have already imperilled the whole success of our expedition. Might I beg that you would have the goodness to sit down upon one of those boxes, and not to interfere?"

The solemn Mr. Merryweather perched himself upon a crate, with a very injured expression upon his face, while Holmes fell upon his knees upon the floor and, with the lantern and a magnifying lens, began to examine minutely the cracks between the stones. A few seconds sufficed to satisfy him, for he sprang to his feet again and put his glass in his pocket.

"We have at least an hour before us," he remarked, "for they can hardly take any steps until the good pawnbroker is safely in bed. Then they will not lose a minute, for the sooner they do their work the longer time they will have for their escape. We are at present, Doctor – as no doubt you have divined – in the cellar of the City branch of one of the principal London banks. Mr. Merryweather is the chairman of directors, and he will explain to you that there are reasons why the more daring criminals of London should take a considerable interest in this cellar at present."

"It is our French gold," whispered the director. "We have had several warnings that an attempt might be made upon it."

"Your French gold?"

"Yes. We had occasion some months ago to strengthen our resources and borrowed for that purpose 30,000 napoleons[81] from the Bank of France. It has become known that we have never had occasion to unpack the money, and that it is still lying in our cellar. The crate upon which I sit contains 2,000 napoleons packed between layers of lead foil. Our reserve of bullion[82] is much larger at present than is usually kept in a

81 A type of gold French coin that issued during the reign of Napoleon I (reigned 1804–15) and features his portrait on one side.

82 Usually means precious metals or coins in bulk for banking purposes.

single branch office, and the directors have had misgivings upon the subject."

"Which were very well justified," observed Holmes. "And now it is time that we arranged our little plans. I expect that within an hour matters will come to a head. In the meantime Mr. Merryweather, we must put the screen over that dark lantern."[83]

"And sit in the dark?"

"I am afraid so. I had brought a pack of cards in my pocket, and I thought that, as we were a *partie carrée*,[84] you might have your rubber after all. But I see that the enemy's preparations have gone so far that we cannot risk the presence of a light. And, first of all, we must choose our positions. These are daring men, and though we shall take them at a disadvantage, they may do us some harm unless we are careful. I shall stand behind this crate, and do you conceal yourselves behind those. Then, when I flash a light upon them, close in swiftly. If they fire, Watson, have no compunction about shooting them down."

I placed my revolver, cocked, upon the top of the wooden case behind which I crouched. Holmes shot the slide across the front of his lantern and left us in pitch darkness – such an absolute darkness as I have never before experienced. The smell of hot metal remained to assure us that the light was still there, ready to flash out at a moment's notice. To me, with my nerves worked up to a pitch of expectancy, there was something depressing and subduing in the sudden gloom, and in the cold dank air of the vault.

"They have but one retreat," whispered Holmes. "That is back through the house into Saxe-Coburg Square. I hope that you have done what I asked you, Jones?"

83 A dark lantern has an integrated screen that can be lowered to obscure the lantern's flame.

84 From the French for a "square party", that is a group of four people.

"I have an inspector and two officers waiting at the front door."

"Then we have stopped all the holes. And now we must be silent and wait."

What a time it seemed! From comparing notes afterwards it was but an hour and a quarter, yet it appeared to me that the night must have almost gone, and the dawn be breaking above us. My limbs were weary and stiff, for I feared to change my position; yet my nerves were worked up to the highest pitch of tension, and my hearing was so acute that I could not only hear the gentle breathing of my companions, but I could distinguish the deeper, heavier in-breath of the bulky Jones from the thin, sighing note of the bank director. From my position I could look over the case in the direction of the floor. Suddenly my eyes caught the glint of a light.

At first it was but a lurid spark upon the stone pavement. Then it lengthened out until it became a yellow line, and then, without any warning or sound, a gash seemed to open and a hand appeared, a white, almost womanly hand, which felt about in the centre of the little area of light. For a minute or more the hand, with its writhing fingers, protruded out of the floor. Then it was withdrawn as suddenly as it appeared, and all was dark again save the single lurid spark which marked a chink between the stones.

Its disappearance, however, was but momentary. With a rending, tearing sound, one of the broad, white stones turned over upon its side and left a square, gaping hole, through which streamed the light of a lantern. Over the edge there peeped a clean-cut, boyish face, which looked keenly about it, and then, with a hand on either side of the aperture, drew itself shoulder-high and waist-high, until one knee rested upon the edge. In another instant he stood at the side of the hole and was hauling after him a companion, lithe and small like himself, with a pale face and a shock of very red hair.

"It's all clear," he whispered. "Have you the chisel and the bags? Great Scott![85] Jump, Archie, jump, and I'll swing for it!"[86]

Sherlock Holmes had sprung out and seized the intruder by the collar. The other dived down the hole, and I heard the sound of rending cloth as Jones clutched at his skirts.[87] The light flashed upon the barrel of a revolver, but Holmes's hunting crop came down on the man's wrist, and the pistol clinked upon the stone floor.

"It's no use, John Clay," said Holmes blandly. "You have no chance at all."

"So I see," the other answered with the utmost coolness. "I fancy that my pal is all right, though I see you have got his coat-tails."

"There are three men waiting for him at the door," said Holmes.

"Oh, indeed! You seem to have done the thing very completely. I must compliment you."

"And I you," Holmes answered. "Your red-headed idea was very new and effective."

"You'll see your pal again presently," said Jones. "He's quicker at climbing down holes than I am. Just hold out while I fix the derbies."[88]

"I beg that you will not touch me with your filthy hands," remarked our prisoner as the handcuffs clattered upon his wrists. "You may not be aware that I have royal blood in my veins. Have the goodness, also, when you address me always to say 'sir' and 'please.' "

"All right," said Jones with a stare and a snigger. "Well, would you please, sir, march upstairs, where we can get a cab to carry your Highness to the police-station?"

---

85 A now archaic exclamation of surprise. Its origin is uncertain.

86 "I'll swing for it" indicates that he thinks he will be hanged if captured.

87 Coat-tails.

88 Derbies was another slang word for handcuffs.

"That is better," said John Clay serenely. He made a sweeping bow to the three of us and walked quietly off in the custody of the detective.

"Really, Mr. Holmes," said Mr. Merryweather as we followed them from the cellar, "I do not know how the bank can thank you or repay you. There is no doubt that you have detected and defeated in the most complete manner one of the most determined attempts at bank robbery that have ever come within my experience."

"I have had one or two little scores of my own to settle with Mr. John Clay," said Holmes. "I have been at some small expense over this matter, which I shall expect the bank to refund, but beyond that I am amply repaid by having had an experience which is in many ways unique, and by hearing the very remarkable narrative of the Red-Headed League."

"You see, Watson," he explained in the early hours of the morning as we sat over a glass of whisky[89] and soda in Baker Street, "it was perfectly obvious from the first that the only possible object of this rather fantastic business of the advertisement of the League, and the copying of the *Encyclopaedia*, must be to get this not over-bright pawnbroker out of the way for a number of hours every day. It was a curious way of managing it, but, really, it would be difficult to suggest a better. The method was no doubt suggested to Clay's ingenious mind by the colour of his accomplice's hair. The £4 a week was a lure which must draw him, and what was it to them, who were playing for thousands? They put in the advertisement, one rogue has the temporary office, the other rogue incites the man to apply for it, and together they manage to secure his absence every morning in the week. From the time that I heard of the assistant having come for half wages, it was

89 In British English this spelling indicates that it was Scotch whisky being consumed. The Irish and American versions are usually spelled "whiskey".

obvious to me that he had some strong motive for securing the situation."

"But how could you guess what the motive was?"

"Had there been women in the house, I should have suspected a mere vulgar intrigue. That, however, was out of the question. The man's business was a small one, and there was nothing in his house which could account for such elaborate preparations, and such an expenditure as they were at. It must, then, be something out of the house. What could it be? I thought of the assistant's fondness for photography, and his trick of vanishing into the cellar. The cellar! There was the end of this tangled clue. Then I made inquiries as to this mysterious assistant and found that I had to deal with one of the coolest and most daring criminals in London. He was doing something in the cellar – something which took many hours a day for months on end. What could it be, once more? I could think of nothing save that he was running a tunnel to some other building.

"So far I had got when we went to visit the scene of action. I surprised you by beating upon the pavement with my stick. I was ascertaining whether the cellar stretched out in front or behind. It was not in front. Then I rang the bell, and, as I hoped, the assistant answered it. We have had some skirmishes, but we had never set eyes upon each other before. I hardly looked at his face. His knees were what I wished to see. You must yourself have remarked how worn, wrinkled, and stained they were. They spoke of those hours of burrowing. The only remaining point was what they were burrowing for. I walked round the corner, saw the City and Suburban Bank abutted on our friend's premises, and felt that I had solved my problem. When you drove home after the concert I called upon Scotland Yard and upon the chairman of the bank directors, with the result that you have seen."

"And how could you tell that they would make their attempt tonight?" I asked.

"Well, when they closed their League offices that was a sign that they cared no longer about Mr. Jabez Wilson's presence – in other words, that they had completed their tunnel. But it was essential that they should use it soon, as it might be discovered, or the bullion might be removed. Saturday would suit them better than any other day, as it would give them two days for their escape. For all these reasons I expected them to come tonight."

"You reasoned it out beautifully," I exclaimed in unfeigned admiration. "It is so long a chain, and yet every link rings true."

"It saved me from ennui,"[90] he answered, yawning. "Alas! I already feel it closing in upon me. My life is spent in one long effort to escape from the commonplaces of existence. These little problems help me to do so."

"And you are a benefactor of the race," said I.

He shrugged his shoulders. "Well, perhaps, after all, it is of some little use," he remarked. " '*L'homme c'est rien – l'oeuvre c'est tout*,'[91] as Gustave Flaubert wrote to George Sand."[92]

---

90 Boredom; derived from the French word.

91 Correctly "*l'homme n'est rien, l'oeuvre tout!*"; "The man is nothing, the work is everything." Perhaps we can forgive Holmes this mistake. In the first Sherlock Holmes book, *A Study in Scarlet*, Watson outlines his friend's limits and states, among others things "Knowledge of Literature – Nothing; Knowledge of Philosophy – Nothing; Knowledge of Politics – Feeble."

92 Gustave Flaubert (1821–80) was a French novelist still held in wide regard. George Sand was the pseudonym for Amantine Dupin (1804–76), a French novelist famous for wearing men's clothing and adopting a masculine demeanour.

Printed in Great Britain
by Amazon

44241378R00024